THE
GREEN SLIME

SUSAN SAUNDERS

ILLUSTRATED BY PAUL GRANGER

An R. A. Montgomery Book

A BANTAM SKYLARK BOOK®
TORONTO · NEW YORK · LONDON · SYDNEY

RL2, 007-009

THE GREEN SLIME

A Bantam Skylark Book / November 1982

CHOOSE YOUR OWN ADVENTURE® is a registered
trademark of Bantam Books, Inc.

Original Conception of Edward Packard

Skylark Books is a registered trademark of Bantam Books, Inc.,
Registered in U.S. Patent and Trademark Office and elsewhere.

Published simultaneously in hardcover and Skylark editions
by Bantam Books November 1982

Library of Congress Cataloging in Publication Data
Saunders, Susan.
The green slime.
(Choose your own adventure)
An "R. A. Montgomery book."
Summary: The reader is given choices to make in order to
fight the green slime made from a chemistry set.
[1. Science—Experiments—Fiction.   2. Literary recreations]
I. Granger, Paul, ill.
II. Title.   III. Series.
PZ7.S2577 Gr   1982   [Fic]   82-11473
ISBN 0-553-05032-X
ISBN 0-553-15162-2 (Skylark choose your own
adventure: pbk.)

Published simultaneously in the United States and Canada

PRINTED IN THE UNITED STATES OF AMERICA

0 9 8 7 6 5 4

To Whitty

READ THIS FIRST!!!

Most books are about other people.

This book is about you!

What happens to you depends on what you decide to do.

Do not read this book from the first page through to the last page. Instead, start on page one and read until you come to your first choice. Then turn to the page shown and see what happens.

When you come to the end of a story, go back and start again. Every choice leads to a new adventure.

Are you ready to fight the green slime? Then turn to page one . . . and good luck!

It's the day after your birthday. Your Aunt Beth has given you a chemistry set as a birthday present. She has also left you in charge of your cousin Stevie while she and your mother go to visit a friend.

"Stevie needs a lot of watching," Aunt Beth warns. And she's not kidding. Within five minutes, the kid has broken your model spaceship, glued together all your baseball cards, and stopped up the sink in the bathroom with tissues.

"Sit down on the bed," you tell Stevie. "Don't move, or you'll be sorry."

You open your new chemistry set. You take out some of the test tubes, which are filled with colored powders and liquids, and you start to mix a few together.

Just then the doorbell rings.

Turn to page 2.

2   Before you go downstairs to answer the door, you take a good look at Stevie. He is leaning against your pillow, and his eyes are closed. You think he has fallen asleep on the bed.

Your friend Jan is at the front door. As you stand there talking to her, you hear shrieks and giggles from upstairs.

"Who is *that*?" Jan asks.

You make a face. "It's only my cousin Stevie," you say. "He's four-and-a-half."

"Don't you think you'd better find out what he's doing up there?" Jan asks.

If you say "no," turn to page 8.

If you say "yes," turn to page 12.

4   You and Jan run all the way to the grocery store.

"Ice!" you shout, as you rush inside.

"Ice?" the clerk says. "How much do you want?"

"Enough to fill a house," you answer.

"Come on, kid," the clerk says. "We're busy in here."

"Well, how much have you got?" you ask.

"With what's out front in the case and with what's in back in the freezer, about 300 bags," the clerk says.

"I'll take all of it," you say. "Please deliver it right away. It's an emergency. And charge it to my parents."

It will take you the next five years to pay for this out of your allowance.

You and Jan run back to the house to wait for the delivery man.

Turn to page 18.

6 Maybe you can reach Stevie on the bed. "Plop. Plop-plop. Blurp."

The green slime is bubbling and Stevie is screaming. The noise is so loud you can hardly think.

Halfway between the bed and the window you see a spot on the floor that is still free of green slime. Maybe you could jump from the window to that spot, and then onto the bed to get Stevie.

Holding on to the window frame, you count: "One . . . two . . . three!" . . . and you jump.

Turn to page 17.

8   "No. He's OK. He'll stop in a minute,"
you tell Jan. And you're right. After a while
Stevie does stop. Everything is quiet. Too
quiet.

"Stevie?" you call. "Stevie!" No answer.

"I'd better go see what he's doing," you
say.

Jan follows you. As you reach the stairs,
you hear a funny bubbling noise: "Plop.
Plop-plop-plop . . . Blurp."

"What's that awful smell?" Jan asks.

It is a *terrible* smell: rotten eggs and glue
and . . .

You and Jan stop short. Something is
starting to drip over the top step in big, thick,
green blobs. What has Stevie done now?

Something tells you not to go near the
green stuff. But should you get help? Or
should you try to reach Stevie first?

If you go to get help, turn to page 21.

If you try to reach Stevie, turn to page 32.

Professor Tate is a scientist. Maybe he can help get rid of the green slime. You find him in the laboratory behind his house, looking into a microscope.

"Take a look," he says. "These little critters eat tar, oil slicks . . . you name it."

They look like tiny shrimp. "Would they eat slime?" you ask.

"As long as they can swim through it, they'll eat it," Professor Tate says.

You quickly explain about the green slime. "This bubbling green gunk is spreading all over the house. My little cousin Stevie is trapped upstairs. I'm afraid the slime will eat him for lunch! Will you help us, Professor?"

Turn to page 45.

12 "We'd better see what Stevie's up to," you say.

Jan follows you up the stairs to your room. Stevie is standing on the chair next to your desk. He is stirring something in a dish. There are empty test tubes and a bottle of glue on the floor.

"What are you doing?" you shout.

"Making pudding." Stevie offers you the dish. Inside is something thick, dark green, and very smelly.

"Yuk!" you say. "It's bubbling."

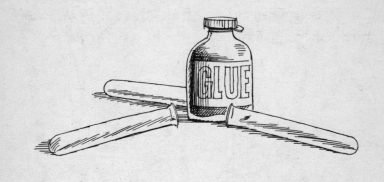

If you say to Stevie, "I ought to spank you,"
turn to page 22.

If you tell Jan to pour it down the sink,
turn to page 31.

14   You get as close to the green slime as you dare. You pour a little of the water in the pail on it. Nothing seems to happen.

"Throw the whole pailful on it!" Jan says.

You dump all the water out. The slime boils and hisses. Then it starts to disappear! You follow it as it disappears through the front door, into the house, and up the stairs.

Now you can see little shrimplike animals swimming around in the green stuff. They're much larger than they were when you first

saw them. And they're getting bigger . . . and **15**
bigger . . . all the time.

"Oh, no!" you say.

"Now what?" Jan says.

"I don't have a good feeling about this," you say.

Turn to page 42.

You jump from the windowsill and land in the empty spot on the floor. But when you try to jump onto the bed, you can't move your feet at all!

You look down. Your feet are now stuck in green slime. And another wave of it is moving toward you. You've got to think fast.

Quickly you untie the laces on your sneakers. You wiggle your feet loose. Then you jump right out of your shoes and onto the bed with Stevie.

Your sneakers are being eaten up by the green slime. "Plop. Slurp." It seems to be enjoying them a lot, especially the bottoms.

The bottoms . . . the bottoms are rubber. Suddenly you have an idea that might get rid of the slime.

But will it work?

The slime is getting deeper on the floor of your room. Should you try your idea? Or should you and Stevie try to get out while you can?

If you try to get out, turn to page 27.

If you try your idea, turn to page 35.

18   When the delivery man gets to your house, you ask him to drive his truck right up to the front door. Jan climbs into the back and starts tearing open the bags of ice.

You grab a shovel and open the front door. Before the green slime can ooze out, you start shoveling the ice inside.

Two hundred ninety-nine bags later, you're finished. It's about thirty degrees inside the house. Your noses have turned blue and you're both shivering. But you've stopped the slime, stopped it cold. It's frozen solid.

Dark green ice covers the floor of your house. Stevie is asleep on your bed. He missed everything.

"What are you going to do with the slime?" Jan wonders.

You think for a minute. "Do you think anyone would buy slime-sicles?"

The End

More and more of the green slime is flowing **21** down the stairs. You couldn't get to Stevie now if you tried. So you decide to go get help.

You and Jan back down the stairs and out of the house.

"Do you think it's . . . alive?" Jan asks. She looks really scared.

You don't feel too great yourself. "Alive or not, we've got to think of some way to stop it. I have an idea that might work. But we've got to hurry," you say, as you start to run.

Jan is right behind you. "Where are we going?" she asks.

If you answer, "To the grocery store,"
turn to page 4.

If you answer, "To Professor Tate's house,"
turn to page 11.

22 Before you know what's happening, Stevie puts the dish to his mouth. You grab it away from him, but it's too late. Stevie has swallowed every drop of the green stuff.

"Yum," he says.

"Oh, no," Jan says. "What if it's poisonous?"

"Do you feel all right?" you ask Stevie.

"Sure," Stevie says. When he opens his mouth, a big green bubble floats out.

"He'll be OK," you say to yourself.

But Jan says, "He's starting to look weird."

Turn to page 39.

24 Like magic, the slime starts to disappear. Soon the whole room is clean.

But you spilled too much of the water while you were climbing the tree. And now it's too late. There aren't enough of the little arimals to eat all of the slime that is pouring down the stairs, through the living room, and out the front door.

As you look out the window, you see a lake of bubbling green stuff growing deeper around your neighbor's house. You wonder where Jan is.

Fountains of slime are coming from the lawn sprinklers up and down the block. A river of slime is oozing slowly down the street.

First your street, then the next one, then the whole town . . . then who knows where —or when—it will stop?

You have to tell everyone that if they hear anything unusual, or smell anything terrible, they had better watch out. Especially if it's *green.*

The End

You've got to get out of your bedroom!

There's a small window at the far end of the room. You can reach it by climbing onto the chest of drawers next to your bed. You swing Stevie onto the chest, then you jump onto it yourself. Next you push the window open and slide out onto the ledge, feet first.

"Come on, Stevie," you say. "I'll catch you."

Stevie closes his eyes and jumps. The green slime is bubbling around the chest now. Stevie's left foot touches it just as you grab him.

Go on to page 28.

28 Luckily, Stevie's shoes aren't tied. You pull as hard as you can on his arms. "Slurp!" His shoe doesn't make it, but Stevie does. You pull him onto the roof ledge beside you.

As you watch, the slime oozes out the windows of the house. It bubbles through the front door and out the back. You are trapped in a lake of gurgling green slime.

Stevie pulls a small bottle out of his pocket. He shakes it hard.

"Give me that!" you shout. "Haven't you caused enough trouble already?" You grab the bottle and pour the purple fizzy stuff over the edge of the roof.

There's a hiss and a "Glop!" from the green slime.

"What was that, Stevie?"

"I made grape drink," he says.

The slime is drying up!

"Can you make more?" you ask Stevie.

"Maybe," he says.

Maybe you will live to see your next birthday after all. You are sure of two things you don't want for your birthday: a chemistry set—and Stevie.

The End

Jan pours the green slimy stuff down the sink in the bathroom—the sink that Stevie stopped up with tissues.

Then she goes downstairs to find a broom and dustpan, to help you clean up the bottles and powders Stevie spilled on the floor. Meanwhile, thick, dark green gunk is bubbling up through the drain.

The sink overflows. Bubbling green slime moves down the hall to your room: "Plop. Plop-plop. Blurp."

"Stop making those funny noises," you say to Stevie. But he is sitting quietly on your bed, taking apart your alarm clock.

What is that sound? It's getting louder. And the smell—it's like a swamp. Suddenly, a river of green glop oozes through your bedroom door. As it moves toward the bed where Stevie is sitting, it starts to bubble louder and jump into the air. Almost as though . . . it would like to get at Stevie?

Turn to page 49.

32   You can't leave Stevie alone with that green slime. Who knows what would happen? You've got to get to him right now.

While Jan keeps an eye on the green gunk coming down the stairs, you climb the oak tree right outside your bedroom window.

On the desk you can see empty test tubes, an empty bottle of glue, and a dish. Green stuff is bubbling in the dish—as if it were trying to get out!

You lean out of the tree and climb onto the window ledge. Now you see that the floor of your room is covered with the bubbling green slime. It seems to be spurting up toward the bed, reaching for . . .

Stevie! He is standing on the bed, crying.

"Stay as far away from the green stuff as you can," you shout. "I'll get you out, Stevie!"

But can you? The bed is pretty far from the window. Can you reach Stevie from here? Or should you climb down the tree and find a ladder?

If you think you can reach Stevie without a
ladder, turn to page 6.

If you climb down to get a ladder,
turn to page 40.

You hope your idea works because there isn't much time. On a shelf above your bed are some rubber swim fins and a rubber mask. You throw them through the door into the hall.

You were right! The slime likes rubber. The slime oozes away from the bed, toward the rubber fins and mask in the hall. "Blurp. Slurp. Plop." It's hungry!

Your room is now clear. You run to your closet and pull out a rubber raft, a basketball, and another pair of sneakers.

"You stay here," you tell Stevie. You go to the door of your bedroom and throw the basketball and sneakers down the stairs. The slime flows down the stairs after them.

Turn to page 46.

36   You decide to pour the water through your bedroom window.

There's a tree at the side of the house. You climb up to the first branch. Jan hands you the pail.

It's hard to climb a tree holding a pail filled with water. As you step from one branch to the next, you spill a little. You lose your balance and spill a little more. And by the time you reach your bedroom window, most of the water in the pail is gone.

You can see Stevie standing on your desk. The green slime is so deep in your room that it reaches almost to the top of the bed.

You must hurry. You grab the pail with both hands and throw it through the window.

Turn to page 24.

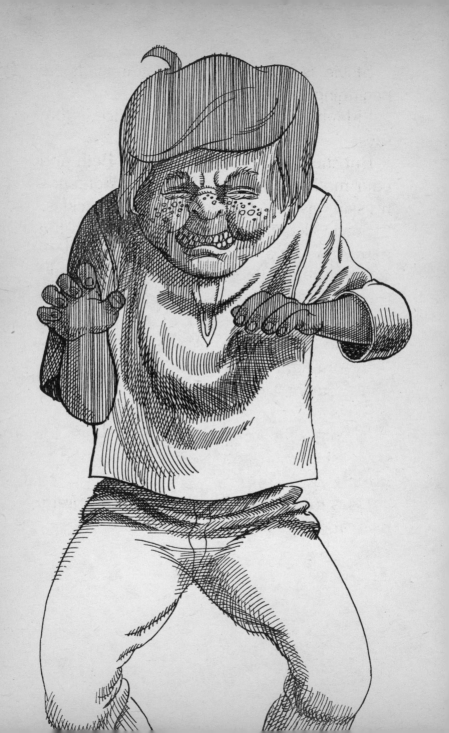

Stevie *is* looking kind of strange. Is he
beginning to turn green?

"Maybe your aunt won't notice," Jan
says.

But she does. By the time Aunt Beth and
your mother get home, Stevie is *all* green—
his skin, his hair, his teeth, even his freckles.

Stevie likes it. He snarls at himself in the
mirror and says, "I'm the Incredible Hulk."

But Aunt Beth is really angry. "Great!"
she says. "Just great! First chicken pox, then
measles, and now this!" She takes Stevie
home to wait for the color to fade.

You hope it fades before your next birthday. Your mother is taking away *this* year's
present.

"I think I'll keep the chemistry set for
you," she says, "until you're old enough to
use it."

Does that seem fair? Stevie used it pretty
well, and he's only four-and-a-half.

The End

40   You climb down the tree to get a ladder. The only ladder you can find in the garage is a very old one with only one rung. "What good is this?" you say to yourself.

You are about to give up when you think: "Stilts!"

You saw the ladder in half. Then you climb up onto the car and step onto your stilts.

They're so high! You rock back and forth, but you think you can do it. You don't see Jan anywhere, but there is a pool of slime all around the house now. It's growing deeper by the minute.

You'll have to walk right through it.

"Slurp. Plop." Somehow you make it to the window. You lean against the house and take a deep breath.

"Stevie," you call. "Climb onto the chest and then through the window."

"No," he whines. "I'll fall."

"Come on, Stevie," you say. "I'll be here to catch you. Pretend you're in a circus."

"Oh, all right," he says.

Turn to page 51.

42   You run up the stairs to your room. Stevie is fast asleep on the bed. But your room is crammed from one end to the other with a big, pale pink shrimp. Its tail is hanging out the window, and it is waving its feelers in a friendly way.

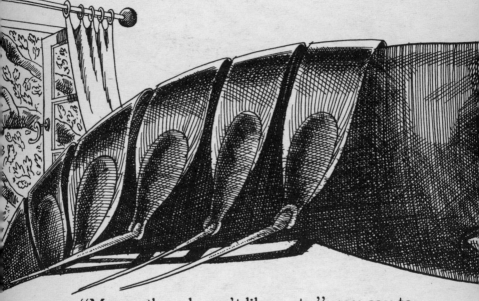

"My mother doesn't like pets," you say to Jan.

"Well, one shrimp is better than a house full of green slime," Jan says.

You nod your head. "Anyway," you say, "I'm sure to win the science fair this year."

The End

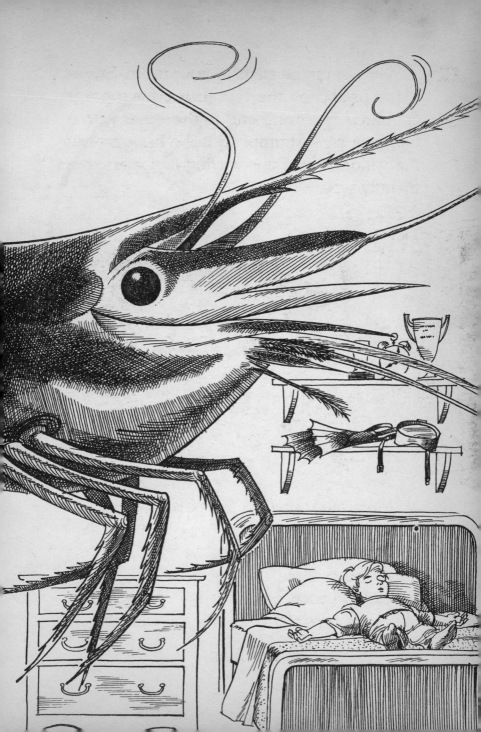

Professor Tate scoops up a pail of water **45**
from a large tank. "There are thousands of the
little fellows in here. This ought to clean up any
kind of mess you have," he says.

There is no time to waste. You and Jan grab
the pail between you and walk as fast as you
can back to your house.

You find the slime oozing under the front
door. Should you pour the pail of water on it
right here and hope the little animals can eat
their way upstairs to your room? Or should
you try to pour the pail of water into your
bedroom, through an upstairs window?

*If you start at the front door,
turn to page 14.*

*If you decide to climb up to your bedroom
window, turn to page 36.*

46 "Look out below!" you shout to Jan, who is somewhere downstairs.

You wait until the slime is busy with the sneakers at the bottom of the stairs. Then you throw the raft through the front door.

Soon the slime is outside. After it eats the raft, it eats the wheels off Jan's bike . . . then the rubber hose in the front yard . . . then the tires off your neighbor's car.

The lake of green slime is growing larger. It's darker and smellier and louder than it was before. "Blurp! Blurp! Gurgle!"

Your idea worked! You got the slime out of your house. You and Stevie and Jan are safe—for now.

But there is something you didn't think of—a way to stop the green slime forever.

The End

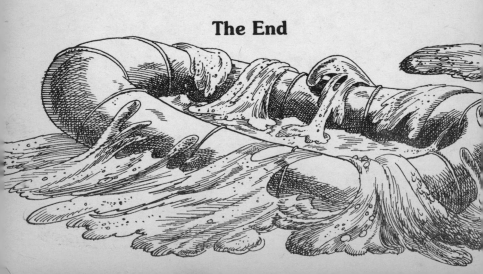

"Stevie!" you shout. "Stay away from that green stuff. It's dangerous!"

Stevie starts to cry. "I want to go home," he screams.

Now the floor of your room is almost covered with green slime. The slime is licking at your toes. You back into the windowsill.

Quickly you turn around, put one foot on the sill, and grab the window frame with both hands. A push and a pull, and you're standing in the window, with a pool of slime gurgling beneath.

"Stevie, hang on," you shout. "I'll get you out of here."

Turn to page 6.

Finally Stevie starts to climb out the bedroom window. You see his head first. Then he sits on the window ledge. "Do what I tell you," you say. "Hold on to the window, and put one foot on my shoulder. Good . . . now grab my head. Now the other foot."

Stevie sits on your shoulders. So far, so good!

"Sit very still," you tell Stevie. You push yourself up straight. You wobble a little on the stilts, but you start to move through the slime.

Go on to page 52.

52   Stevie laughs. "I like this game."

A crowd has gathered around the lake of slime. When you reach the crowd, everyone cheers. A photographer takes a picture of you, Jan, and Stevie.

You're a star. But what about the slime? You see the police setting up roadblocks on the street past your house. There is a helicopter flying overhead.

When is it going to end?

The End

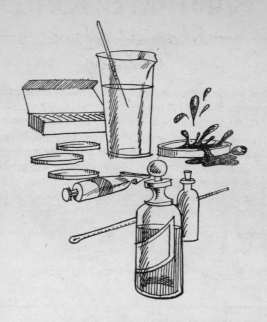

ABOUT THE AUTHOR

Susan Saunders grew up on a ranch in Texas, where she learned rodeo riding. A graduate of Barnard College, she has been a ceramicist and an editor of filmstrips for children. She is the author of *Wales' Tale*, which was a Junior Literary Guild selection; *A Sniff in Time*; and *Fish Fry*. Ms. Saunders currently lives in New York City.

ABOUT THE ILLUSTRATOR

Paul Granger is a prize-winning illustrator and painter.

SAVE $2.00 ON YOUR NEXT BOOK ORDER!

BANTAM BOOKS 🐓
—— *Shop-at-Home* ——
Catalog

Now you can have a complete, up-to-date catalog of Bantam's inventory of over 1,600 titles—including hard-to-find books. And, you can save $2.00 on your next order by taking advantage of the money-saving coupon you'll find in this illustrated catalog. Choose from fiction and non-fiction titles, including mysteries, historical novels, westerns, cookbooks, romances, biographies, family living, health, and more. You'll find a description of most titles. Arranged by categoreis, the catalog makes it easy to find your favorite books and authors and to discover new ones.

So don't delay—send for this shop-at-home catalog and save money on your next book order.

Just send us your name and address and 50¢ to defray postage and handling costs.

BANTAM BOOKS, INC.
Dept. FC, 414 East Golf Road, Des Plaines, Ill. 60016

Mr./Mrs./Miss _____
(please print)

Address _____

City _____ State _____ Zip _____

Do you know someone who enjoys books? Just give us their names and addresses and we'll send them a catalog too at no extra cost!

Mr./Mrs./Miss _____

Address _____

City _____ State _____ Zip _____

Mr./Mrs./Miss _____

Address _____

City _____ State _____ Zip _____

FCSK—4/83

Bantam—FCSK-4/83